Christmas 19[illegible]

To dearest Alice

From Papa & Granny-Mum

TALES FROM THE THREEPENNY BIT

This book belongs to

Alice Dwyer

Tales from the Threepenny Bit

·Wendy Eyton·

Illustrated by Penny Dann

COLLINS

For Yvette, Madeline and Peter,
remembering Oscar and with Wendy's love

William Collins Sons & Co Ltd
London · Glasgow · Sydney · Auckland
Toronto · Johannesburg

First published 1990

A CIP catalogue record for this book is available
from the British Library.

ISBN 0 00 184994-8

Printed and bound in Great Britain by
Hartnolls Ltd, Bodmin, Cornwall

·*Contents*·

1 The House with Golden Windows 7

2 The Magic Thistledown Dog 12

3 The Fairy Pipe 20

4 The Snake and the Rose 25

5 The Princess and the Linnet 30

6 The Prancing Prince 34

7 The Kind Scarecrow 41

8 Tadpole's Dream 46

9 The Rainbow Pearl 50

10 The Fat Princess 56

11 Jinny Greenteeth 61

12 The Kingdom Under the Hill 65

13 The Boggart and the Bakewell Pudding 71

14 The Princess who met the North Wind 78

15 The Woman who grew Butterflies 82

16 The Hagge Tree 86

17 Mouse in the Snow 92

The House with Golden Windows

There was once a man who lived in a dear little cottage, with white doves on the roof and honeysuckle curling around the door. At first the man was very happy in his cottage, but as the years went by he began to be discontented.

Every summer morning the man would fling open his bedroom window and look down upon a garden bright with blossom and buzzing with bees. Then he would look up at the blue distant hills and sigh. For on the farthest hillside stood a magnificent mansion, with towers and turrets and pointed windows. And the panes in all the windows were made of shining gold.

"How wonderful it would be," said the man to himself, "to live in the house with golden windows. There is sure to be a huge ballroom. What wonderful parties I could have. How everyone would envy me."

And he looked at his own window, with its gaily painted frame and dancing curtains. He heard the rose trees tapping their branches on the windowpane and sighed again, most discontentedly.

One morning, the windows of the big house on the hillside seemed to be glowing more brightly and more golden than ever. The man decided he must go to look at the house and find out who was living in it.

"Perhaps," he thought, "I might find work there. A house like that must need servants to look after it – cooks in the kitchen and stable-boys to groom the horses. Or perhaps I could work as a window-cleaner and polish those beautiful golden windows. Who knows, I might earn enough money to buy the house one day."

And he put some bread and cheese into a pack, threw the pack over his shoulder and set off.

After about a mile of walking the man came to a wide, fast-flowing river. The water hurled itself against huge boulders. It tore up the waterweed by its roots – long, green and straggling as witches hair. Bright little fishes leapt and darted in the foaming torrent and the man, who was making a meal of his bread and cheese, threw some pieces of bread to them.

Then the fishes showed the man the biggest and safest boulders, and he stepped from stone to slippery stone and crossed the river safely. But his shoes became loose and were tossed by the current, along with old tin cans and rotting branches of trees.

After resting awhile, the man had to cross a great expanse of moorland. The bracken and heather tore at his bare feet until they bled. At length, tired and weary from hours of walking, he threw himself onto a patch of moss. He drank some water and shared what was left of his bread and cheese with a little bird who was flying overhead.

"The rest is easy," said the man to himself. "Only a green field to cross and a hill to climb and I will reach the house with golden windows."

But when he climbed over the gate and into the field his heart sank. For in the field was a great, black, wicked-looking bull with a brass ring through its nose. When the bull saw the man, who was wearing a red shirt, it narrowed its eyes and lowered its head and began to charge.

The man tore off his shirt and threw it onto the grass. Then he ran this way and that, trying to escape from the horns of the bull. But the little bird who had shared the man's meal fluttered her wings over the head of the bull, so that the bull ran blindly into a bank of mud. Its horns stuck fast in the mud, and the man crossed the field safely.

Without shoes, and with no shirt, the man found climbing the hill very difficult. The hot sun beat against his back and the sharp stones cut his feet and slipped from under them, so that for every step he climbed, he slid down two. The little bird flew overhead and sang a song to cheer his spirit. Wherever there was a clump of grass to hold on to, or a tiny ledge to fit a foot in, she pointed her wings at them.

When the man reached the top of the hill it was almost evening and the sun was sinking fast. Nearly fainting with exhaustion he raised his head to look at the house with golden windows – but all he saw was a ruin!

The steps had crumbled away, the doors had fallen in and the big, black crows flapped in and out of the turrets. The windows were cracked and thick with cobwebs – and they were not made of gold at all!

"Turn round," sang the bird, "and look at what you left behind you!"

The man turned just as the last rays of the setting sun poured across the valley. He saw his own little cottage nestling in its woodland garden, with white doves on the roof and honeysuckle around the doorway – and the setting sun shone on the windows, so that they seemed to be made of gold.

"How foolish I have been," said the man to himself. "For the sun shone on the windows of the big house every morning and on my cottage every evening. My windows were made of gold and I didn't even notice."

* * *

The man ran quickly down the hill and the bird flew with him. He reached the field and rescued the big black bull from the mud, and the bull carried the man across the field, across the moor and over the rushing river, with the fish darting between its legs and the little bird perched on its horns.

The man ran up his garden path and threw open his cottage door with a cry of contentment. Then he thanked the bull and made himself a cup of tea – and the little bird flew off to build a nest in the garden.

The Magic Thistledown Dog

I want to tell you about an old man and woman who lived in a cottage near Matlock wood. The cottage was small, and they had not much money, but they were happy enough. The cottage was always clean and bright, and in the garden they grew potatoes and cabbages and beautiful lemon-coloured roses.

In the autumn the man would go into the wood to pick blackberries and collect sticks for the fire. One day, he heard a tiny cry coming from between the roots of a huge old oak tree. And there, waving at him, was a pixie dressed in a green coat and green pointed hat. The hat had a bright red feather in it.

"Help, help," cried the pixie. "I am trapped between the roots of this oak tree. I can't climb over them and I can't squeeze under them. Will you come over here and lift me out, please?"

To reach the pixie, the man had to step through a patch of thistles that prickled his ankles above his shoes and made them very sore. He pressed and pressed aside the roots of the oak tree, gently lifted out the pixie, and dusted him down. Then he gave him first pick of the bowl of blackberries he had been gathering. When the pixie had eaten his fill of one large blackberry, he thanked the man in his high, sing-song voice.

"Pixies make wishes come true for people who are kind to them," he said. "And you have been very kind to me, old man. Tell me your heart's desire and I will work magic for you."

The man thought long and hard about the wish. He was tempted to ask the pixie to stop his ankles from hurting from the prickles, but he knew that at home, in the cupboard, was a jar of ointment which would work as well, if he were patient about it. He thought of asking for great wealth, but decided he was happier with his wife, in their little cottage.

"There is one thing my wife and I would like," said the man to the pixie. "We would like a little companion to walk with on summer days and cheer us up on winter evenings."

When he had said this, the pixie took the red feather out of his hat and waved it over the patch of thistles. As it was autumn-time, some of the thistles were covered in that soft, white woolly stuff called thistledown. A ball of this thistledown grew and grew until, before the surprised eyes of the man, it turned into a fluffy little white dog, with a black nose and eyes as round and black as the berries the man was holding.

The little dog's tail shot up and curled over his back as tight as a corkscrew. He looked at the man with his blackberry eyes and bared his teeth into what was most certainly a grin. Then he gave a bark, stood up on his back legs and plunged off into the undergrowth.

"Don't go! Come back here!" shouted the man, and he followed the little dog with never a thought for the pixie.

When they arrived home the man's wife was working at her wooden spinning-wheel, spinning loose wool into yarn for a neighbouring farmer. When she saw the little dog, she stopped spinning at once.

"Why, what have we here?" she cried. "Are you a little dog or a little lamb or what?"

She bent down and hugged the little fellow, then hurried to the kitchen to find him something to eat.

From that day, the little dog stayed with the old man and woman and they were all very happy together. The man and woman fed him well, and in return the little dog guarded the house. He went for walks through the wood with them, and played with the squirrels and rabbits. And at night, when they all sat together around a crackling log fire, the little dog would roll over with a sigh of contentment, stick his legs in the air, show his tummy and grin.

"He really has the most wonderful white wool," said the woman, stroking him. "Far better than any of the sheeps' wool the farmer gives me to spin. And look how it's growing. We never need fear that our little white dog will feel the cold winter winds."

But spring came early that year, with a sudden warm spell that brought out the celandines and bluebells, and even a bumble-bee or two. The little dog was feeling very hot in his woolly coat, so, while the man held him still, the woman took up a pair of long, sharp scissors and snip-snipped, ever so gently, at the soft white wool which floated to the floor like finest thistledown.

The strange thing was, the more she snipped, the more the wool seemed to grow. Soon the room was full of it – like soft, floating clouds. Only when the man and woman had packed it all into a bag, and filled the bag many times over, did the little dog's wool stop growing – and he looked a bit like a shorn sheep. Then he started to frolic about, and show how pleased he was. And a little bird who had perched on the windowsill caught a piece of the wool in her beak and flew off to line her nest with it.

The man washed all the wool from the little white dog, and spread it to dry in the sunshine. And that evening, instead of spinning wool from the farmer's sheep, the woman started to spin the little dog's wool. She worked night after night and soon had piles of the softest, whitest yarn.

By the time winter came round again, she had

knitted the yarn into the most beautiful coverlet that had ever been seen in that part of the country. The man and woman put the coverlet on their bed and found it warmer than toast and lighter than a feather. All their neighbours came to admire it, and the little white dog lay down on top of it and snored.

But there was one man in the village who not only admired the coverlet, but wanted one for himself. This man was called Bad Jem, and he lived on an acre of land in a broken-down caravan.

Bad Jem was not kind to animals. He set a rabbit-trap in the wood, and one dark night he stepped into it, which everyone said was justice. He tried keeping hens, but fed them so badly they all ran away. And it was this Jem who lay in wait in the wood for the little white dog, threw an old blanket over him and carried him off to a hut, which no one knew was there, on the acre of land at the back of his caravan.

There was one small window in the hut, high up and dirty, and very little light came through. The air in the hut was cold and damp. Bad Jem tied the little white dog to a post in a corner and gave him only a heap of filthy straw to sleep on. He tossed him scraps of bone and gristle and more often than not forgot to fill his water dish. The little dog thought of the old man and woman, and how they would be missing him, and tears trickled from his deep, soulful blackberry eyes down to his blackberry nose. But still the spell kept working and his coat kept growing – and there was a reason for this, as you will see.

The old man and woman were heart-broken at losing their little companion. They combed the countryside in search of him and hung notices on the trees promising rewards for his return. But they did not once think of Bad Jem and his acre of land behind the broken-down caravan.

Weeks passed, and Bad Jem went to the village shop and bought himself a pair of the longest, sharpest scissors. He shouted at the little white dog as he cut and hacked at the wool. The little dog stood very still, for he knew Jem would poke his eye out as soon as look at him.

Soon the hut was filled with floating clouds of softest wool, as the old couple's room had been. Bad Jem jumped for joy.

"I will keep you forever," he told the little white dog. "And I will make coverlets to sell every week at the market. Soon I will be a rich man."

The little dog's tail, which had not curled like a corkscrew since the day Bad Jem made off with him, now disappeared completely between his back legs and looked as if it would never come up again.

Bad Jem collected together all the wool but, being Jem, he did not think of washing it. He carried a broken-down old spinning-wheel into the hut and tried to spin the wool, but the first thing he did was to prick his finger.

There are some people who, when misfortune hits them, have to make others unhappy too – and Jem was one of those people. Hopping about with pain he picked up a big stick and was just about to hit the little dog with it when there was a flash of green up at the tiny window. Jem turned in amazement to see the pixie sitting there.

"Drop that stick," ordered the pixie. "Or I will turn you into a jelly baby."

Jem dropped the stick at once.

"I ought to turn you into one anyway," continued the pixie. "This little dog is a friend of mine and you have treated him shamefully. But if you make amends, and set him free, I will wave the feather from my hat and turn the pile of wool you are sitting on into a wonderful coverlet. I can't say fairer than that, can I?"

Jem shook his head, thinking secretly that he could always kidnap the little dog again, when the pixie was far away. He untied the rope from the little white dog's neck and the little dog stretched his legs painfully and hobbled to the door. Then he started to run across the field, getting stronger and stronger, until he reached the cottage where his two old friends lived.

How they cried with joy to see him, and patted him and hugged him, I hardly need to tell you. The little white dog had the best meal of his life that evening – tasty meat stew with cabbage and herbs, special biscuits and a dish of pure spring water. Then he went upstairs and stretched out on the wool coverlet and snored happily. The old man and woman crept into bed and snored happily too.

And what of Bad Jem?

Back at his broken-down caravan he, too, was planning to step inside a coverlet – the wonderful wool coverlet which had appeared when the pixie waved his feather over the pile of the little dog's wool. And, except for the old couple's coverlet, it was the softest, lightest one in the world for, as you will have guessed by now, the little white dog was a magic dog and his wool was not really wool but the softest thistledown.

And so it was with the greatest anticipation that Bad Jem threw off all his clothes and climbed into bed and snuggled down under the coverlet.

But as soon as he did so, the thistledown turned back into *thistles* – the prickliest, deadliest thistles imaginable.

"Ow! . . . Ooh! . . . Ahh! . . . Help! . . . Save me!" cried Bad Jem.

But though he shouted and struggled and kicked, no one heard him. And the more he struggled and kicked the more he became entangled with the prickles. And the more they pricked his arms and legs and buttocks, until they were red raw, the louder he yelled.

And he never, *ever*, tried to steal the little white dog again.

The Fairy Pipe

A farm worker was digging in a field when he turned up a small clay pipe.

"Hello, what's this?" said the man, whose name was Alfred.

As it was nearly time for his dinner, Alfred put down his spade, wiped his hands and made a hearty meal of his cheese and beetroot sandwiches. Then he had a drink of tea from his flask and picked up the pipe for a closer look. It was perfectly formed and on the outside was the faintest tracing of an oak-leaf pattern.

"Bless me," said Alfred, "if it isn't a fairy pipe."

Alfred cleaned the soil from the bowl of the pipe. He filled it with tobacco from the leather pouch which he carried in his green jacket pocket. Then he leaned back against a rock and surveyed the wonderful sweep of sky and hill and moorland, puffing contentedly.

"If this isn't the sweetest baccy I've ever tasted," he said, and then he sniffed the air with delight. The scent that came from the pipe was of roses and violets and peppermint and newmown hay, all mingled together in one fragrance.

As the bowl of the pipe was so small, Alfred had soon smoked all the tobacco away. But the sun was warm and he was well on with his work, so he decided to fill it up again.

"Puff puff," went Alfred, sucking away at the stem of his pipe, and as he did so a strange thing happened. A film passed over his eyes so that he could no longer see the hills and moorland – or even the midday sun which had been shining so brightly. Then the film lifted and in front of him, beneath a large stone, the ground became transparent and Alfred could see down, far below the surface of the earth, a fairy kingdom.

He saw mountains of crystal, snow-capped, and palaces made of mirrors.

He saw trees of glistening silver and birds with golden plumage nesting in them.

He saw fairy people dressed in gossamer and silk, and milk-white horses with diamond hooves and a peacock with one eye like a great red ruby.

How long Alfred gazed at this beautiful scene I do not know, but bit by bit the film came back across his eyes and a feeling of soreness made him rub them. Then his pipe went out and he saw the hillside as it had been before, except that the sun was sinking fast into the west and he knew that he should have been home hours ago.

"You're late," his wife snapped, as soon as he walked through the doorway of their cottage. "There's the coal to fetch, the hens to feed and the gate to mend or there'll be no supper for you tonight."

She was surprised that instead of arguing he did all the jobs asked of him, and she saw a faraway look in his eyes and wondered at it.

Day after day, when his morning's work was done, Alfred would sit on the turf by the rock, take out his tobacco and fill the fairy pipe. And each time the film would come over his eyes and when it cleared he saw underground the shining mountains and palaces, the glittering trees, the fairy people and milk-white horses, the peacock with the ruby eye, and many more things too wonderful to describe.

But his work in the fields was beginning to suffer, and as he arrived home in the evening later and later his wife became crosser and crosser. But still she wondered at his gentle manner and the faraway look in his eyes.

One morning, the man left behind his green jacket for washing and wore his other jacket for working in the fields. He forgot to take the tobacco pouch and the pipe from the pocket of the green jacket and his wife found them there. She caught a whiff of roses, violets, peppermint and newmown hay.

"So that's it," said the wife to herself. "A fairy pipe! That explains everything. He's been lying around smoking this when he should have been working in the fields. Well, two can play at that game!"

And she dumped her washing in the copper boiler, sat on a kitchen stool, stuffed the bowl of the pipe with tobacco and began to smoke it.

A film came across her eyes. The kitchen shelves, the shining pans, the line of washing over the fire, all faded into the distance. Then the film cleared, and in front of her the floor became transparent and down, down under the brown linoleum she saw another kingdom.

She saw mountains of old cheese, topped with mould, and heaps of cracked, distorted mirrors.

She saw glistening cobwebs with black, hairy spiders hanging upside down in them.

She saw thin, bony people dressed in rags, shaggy ponies pulling dustcarts and a rat with one eye which glowed wickedly like a great red lump of coal.

Alfred's wife screamed and beat her fists on the kitchen table. The pipe broke in two, fell to the floor, and she stamped on the broken pieces. The room returned to normal suddenly, in a blinding flash, and she threw the pieces of pipe onto the fire and shovelled lump after lump of coal on top of them.

* * *

When Alfred came home and found out what had happened, he shouted at his wife in anger, and then he wept.

In the years that followed he never dug up a spadeful of soil, or scythed a blade of grass, without expecting to see a fairy pipe on the ground before him.

But he never found another.

The Snake and the Rose

One hot day in high summer, Snake lay basking on the stone steps which led down to the garden. He lay uncurled at the top of the steps and listened to the chattering of the flowers.

The Marigolds were laughing prettily together, smiling their golden smiles. "Whoever heard of a *snake* falling in love with a *rose*? It's too absurd," said one to another.

"He *is* a very handsome snake," said the Forget-me-not wistfully, "in his shining, silver armour."

The Pansy blinked her purple eye and gazed up at the rose-tree where a perfect rose, the colour of dark red velvet, blushed to a scarlet hue and pretended not to hear what the other flowers were saying about her.

"Hoity-toity!" laughed the Marigold. "She can

afford to be, with the Snake at her beck and call, driving away all those nasty snails and slugs."

The Snake was, indeed, very much in love with the beautiful, red Rose, and all through the summer he had been protecting her. But as the sun's rays grew hotter and hotter he found it more and more difficult to move. The flowers, too, began to wilt and hang their heads, and soon even the Marigolds were silent.

As dusk fell, the Snake dragged himself to his hole in the wall and lay there, panting. His skin felt as dry as parchment paper. There was a click of the gate and the woman from the house climbed down the steps with a watering can. She sprinkled the water over the heads of the Marigolds, Forget-me-nots and Pansies. Then she turned to the Rose and gave her a cooling spray. The Rose reached towards the drops of silver water, her petals forming a cup.

When the woman returned to the house the Rose still held a pool of shining water. She called softly to the Snake who, pushing his slack body against stones and sticks, slowly came to her. The Rose leaned towards the Snake carefully, so as not to spill the precious water. The Snake drank and drank his fill and for a moment rested his throat on her curved, diamond-spattered petals.

From that time he loved her more than ever. Each day he would protect the Rose and each evening, after foraging for food, he would sleep by her, winding his silver body around the rose-tree and resting his head on her petalled cheek.

But one evening the weather changed, with a chill wind blowing. The Snake, shivering a little, went as usual to see his Rose, but she was not there. He searched high and low, but could not find her. A Marigold, whose sleep he had disturbed, said crossly, "The woman from the house has picked her. Taken her into a nice warm room, I shouldn't wonder. Some flowers have all the luck."

And the wind ruffled her petals and sang its song through the branches of the damson tree.

The Snake waited until all was still inside the house and the lights were switched off. Then he pushed his body up the steps, underneath the gate and along the pavement until at last he came to the door.

The door of the house had a gap at the bottom, and the Snake wriggled through the gap and into the room on the other side. His soft belly felt the roughness of a carpet. On the table, in a blue Japanese vase, was the Rose. She smiled to see him, and then wept a few petals onto the polished surface of the table.

"How I wish," said the Rose, "that I was back with you in the garden. I cannot breathe in here. The air is stifling. Soon all my petals will be gone."

The Snake did what he could to comfort her, but when daylight came the Rose begged him to leave.

He promised to visit her every night, and slipped back under the door.

For three nights the Snake visited the Rose, and each time he saw her she wept a few more petals. One morning, the woman from the house took what was left of the Rose and threw her onto a mossy bank, which lay between the bottom of the garden and a dark, mysterious wood.

The Snake slid down from his wall, crossed the garden and gazed at the withered Rose. He felt as if his heart was breaking. When night fell, he burrowed sadly under the moss and dead leaves, under the crumpled dark red petals, and fell into a deep sleep which was almost like death itself.

The summer days had ended and soon winter rains battered all the golden-brown leaves from the trees. The chattering of the flowers had long ceased, and the chorus of birdsong gave way to the strange, wild cry of the owl. Snow fell, layer upon layer, and the earth was hushed and still.

When spring rains came, melting the snow, there was a stirring in the mossy bank between the garden and the wood. When the spring sun shone and flowers danced in the breeze, the Snake came warily into the open again. He warmed himself on the stone slabs and listened to the cooing of the grey collared Dove. The Primroses talked to him, but still his heart was sad.

Spring deepened into summer and the Snake went back to the rose-tree. It was showing fresh green leaves now, and on the branch where his Rose had been, a tiny bud was forming. The Snake gazed at the bud longingly and whispered to it, but the bud did not reply.

Day after day the Snake visited the rose-tree and, one warm and glorious morning, the bud burst into petals of velvet red. Then the Snake knew that after the long winter months the Rose had returned to him, and his heart was filled with happiness and joy.

The Princess and the Linnet

Once upon a time there was a princess with hair as fine and yellow as spun gold. Sometimes she wore her hair braided into plaits and sometimes she wore it loose and straight, down her back as far as her waist.

"It drops to her waist like a golden waterfall," said her father, the old king. But when he fondly stroked his daughter's golden locks his wife, the stepmother of the princess, pushed his hand away roughly. For the stepmother was jealous of the princess and her long, golden hair. She herself was tall as a tree, with hair as black as night and eyes as black as jet.

When the old king died, his wife locked the princess in a high, narrow tower, without food or drink, and hid the key to the tower inside her palace. The only company the princess had was a linnet in a cage.

When the princess wept, the small brown bird sang sweetly to cheer her. But after two days in the tower the princess became pale and faint with hunger and thirst and fell to the floor.

The dreamy song of the linnet changed to an urgent twittering. He beat his wings against the door of the cage until it swung open. The linnet flew twice around the turret room, and then out of a small pointed window high in the eaves.

Near to the turret of the tower grew a magic tree, with tinkling silver leaves, snow-white flowers and purple fruits. The linnet plucked a fruit from the tree and carried it back to the princess.

When she had eaten the fruit the princess felt less dizzy and could stand on her feet again. And, to her surprise, she could understand the words of the song the linnet was singing to her.

"Outside your window is a magic tree," sang the linnet. "It bears leaves and fruits and flowers all year long. The fruits have magic in them. If you eat just one magic fruit each day, you will be strong and healthy."

And, throughout the cold winter months, the linnet flew each day to the magic tree and plucked a fruit for the princess. And he passed the long hours by singing beautiful songs to her, and telling her tales of the gorsey heathland where he was born, of the distant blue mountains, and mysterious forests where giant moths and fairies flew.

* * *

But throughout those winter months the stepmother of the princess ruled her kingdom with a rod of iron. If any person dared to ask the fate of the princess, she banished that person on pain of death. She took money and goods from the poor, even though they had no shoes to walk in. And with the money she bought ever more costly jewels for the crown she always wore on her jet-black hair.

"We shiver with cold, our animals are sick and our children are starving," cried the people of the kingdom. But the rubies and pearls and amethysts glowed in the crown of the wicked queen, as she shook her head and laughed at their discomfort.

Spring came at last. The linnet was showing his fine crimson feathers and the cheeks of the princess were round and rosy, too.

"You have been a dear friend to me throughout the winter," said the princess to the little bird, kissing him. "But now that spring is here you must fly away and build a nest for yourself. Take this gift from me – then you will have the finest nest in the forest."

And she cut off all her golden hair, and gave it to the linnet to build his nest with.

The linnet flew to the magic tree with the long strands of yellow hair in his beak, and he built a nest amongst the snow white flowers, purple fruits and tinkling silver leaves and branches. When he had finished the nest, the little bird flew into it.

And the nest became a golden crown and the

linnet became a handsome prince, who kissed his hand to the princess at the turret window, climbed down the tree and made his way to the palace.

The wicked queen was delighted to see a handsome young prince at her palace door. She decided then and there to marry him, and when the prince asked for the key to the tower she gave it to him, thinking that the princess would have died long before.

She called a meeting of all the people of her kingdom who came, barefoot and in patched clothes, to hear of the sumptuous wedding she planned with her young bridegroom. And as she was telling them of all the pheasants and goose-eggs and roasting-pigs she would need for the wedding feast, in walked the prince with the princess, who was looking well and bonny – and as pretty as ever, despite the fact that she had cut off her hair.

The wicked queen clenched her fists and gave a cry of rage – and as she did so the crown of shining jewels on her head turned into an old birds' nest, with bits of straw sticking out of it, and soft mud which ran down her face and into her eyes.

When the people saw that the queen was wearing, not a crown, but a bird's nest, they chased her from the palace, across the fields and out of the kingdom for ever.

The prince and princess sold the palace and built a cottage under the magic tree.

And they were very happy there, and the people prospered.

The Prancing Prince

There was once a prince who loved to dress up in bright, colourful costumes and comb out his curly golden locks until they shone in the glow from the palace chandeliers. He liked to dance the minuet, and play croquet, but he was not interested in killing dragons, or chasing away monsters, or rescuing princesses, or anything like that.

"When I was your age," grumbled the king, "I would think nothing of killing seven dragons before breakfast."

"One, dear," put in the queen mildly. "And that was a very old one, and just before lunch."

The king picked up a copy of the Court Gazette and waved the pages of the newspaper at the prince, who was dangling cherries over his ears.

"A pearly-toothed princess has been locked inside a high tower by a wicked wizard," said the king.

"He cast a spell on her several months ago. The tower is surrounded by a moat and drawbridge, and the moat is guarded by an immense fiery dragon."

"Dear, dear," murmured the queen, putting on her reading spectacles. "It says that to break the wizard's spell a brave prince must overcome the fiery dragon, cross the moat and vanquish the Green-Eyed Goggle that guards the door to the tower. Whatever do you suppose a green-eyed goggle is?"

The king did not know, but he was determined that the prince was going to find out.

"You will never be fit to rule my kingdom unless you kill a few dragons and rescue a few princesses," he told his son. "And this sounds as easy a first job as any."

And he told the prince to be up at dawn and ready to set out on his quest as soon as possible.

But the prince did not roll out of bed until eleven o'clock, and then he could not find a suit of armour to fit him.

"It's so ugly and so un*comfor*table," he complained, clanking about the palace corridors. "I can't bend my knees and I can't bend my arms and I can't see where I'm going. Oh, *drat* the thing."

And he threw off every bit of armour and dressed himself most carefully in the latest craze in tights, with one of his legs covered in bright red wool and the other in bright yellow. Then he put on a doublet and shoes of softest leather, with toes twelve inches long that curled up at the ends, mounted his horse with some difficulty and rode out of the palace gates.

To reach the tower where the princess was held prisoner, the prince had to cross many miles of rolling countryside. He was not a good horseman at the best of times, but to urge the animal on was nearly impossible, because he was wearing such silly shoes. And the horse refused to jump over ditches and wanted to stop at every stream for a long, cool drink and at every hedgerow for a tasty nibble.

At last the prince, utterly fed up, climbed off his horse and gave it a slap on the rump that sent it cantering back to the palace. But after half an hour he wished he had not done so, for the soft rolling hillside gave way to rough moorland, and the gorse and bracken pricked the prince's feet through his soft leather shoes, and tore his tights until they hung in shreds.

Complaining and muttering, the prince, at long last, spied in the distance a high, turreted tower, surrounded by a shining moat. And there, sure enough, guarding the drawbridge, was a dragon. The newspaper had exaggerated, as usual, and the dragon was not all that immense, but he was quite fiery, and the grass beneath his feet was scorched black and brown.

"Hold it!" cried the prince in a quavering voice

and then, remembering that he had not brought any weapon, was about to run.

But at the sight of him the dragon started to roar, not with anger but with laughter, and he laughed so much that salty tears ran in rivulets down his hoary cheeks and, in no time at all, the dragon's fiery breath had fizzled into a single plume of thin, grey smoke and disappeared. Then the dragon lumbered away from the blackened grass at his feet, sniffed at the sweeter grass in the meadow and started munching it. He took no more notice of the prince, who darted round behind him and managed to lower the drawbridge, but not without hurting his back and breaking his fingernails, which made him very cross.

The Green-Eyed Goggle, that guarded the tower door, was every bit as hideous as could be expected. It had one huge eye in the centre of its forehead, and the eye was green and glaring with thousands of different sides to it, the way a fly's eye has. Legend said that if the Green-Eyed Goggle stared at you for sixty seconds you would turn to stone for the next ten years – and, certainly, there were stone statues all over the place.

The prince stood his ground and raised his eyeglass to look at the goggle, not because he was brave, but because he was short-sighted and had not received the full impact of the hideous thing. But the Goggle was fascinated by the eyeglass, that hung on a gold chain around the prince's neck, and it made all sorts of repulsive sounds like "Gimme-GimmeGimme," and put out its knobbly fist. The prince held onto the eyeglass, because he could not understand goggle language, but the creature snatched the glass and chain away from him, and threw down an iron key in exchange.

While the Goggle played with the eyeglass, the prince unlocked the door of the tower with the heavy iron key, puffing at the stiffness of it, and ran up the stone steps inside the tower – hundreds and hundreds of them – until he thought his knees would cave in.

The princess had lovely pearly teeth it is true, but she showed them in an unfriendly scowl when the prince, panting and dishevelled, burst through her chamber door. Collapsing onto a silk-fringed stool, the prince explained that he had come a long way and faced many dangers to rescue her from the wizard's spell.

"But I can't come yet," pouted the princess, who was busy with her embroidery frame. "There's still a leaf and a bluebird to do."

"Well, bring the embroidery with you," urged the prince. "We must get away before the dragon stops eating grass and the Goggle gets tired of its new plaything."

He led the princess gently to the top of the stairs, but after going down two or three steps, she protested so much about how steep they were and how slippery they were, and how her dress was getting dirty, that he had to take her back to the tower again. Then he ran downstairs and out of the tower, past the Goggle, who was looking through the glass with the hundredth side of its great eye – and up to the dragon to ask if he would do him a favour.

"Anything, dear chap," said the dragon. "It was so good of you to put my fire out. The grass hasn't tasted so fresh for years."

So he allowed the prince to climb onto his back, and they rose up, up into the air to rescue the princess from her pointed turret window.

But when the princess saw the great beast flapping about outside, she ran to the other end of the chamber, pressed herself against the wall and screamed at the prince that she liked living in a tower and working on her embroidery frame, and just wanted to be left alone.

So the prince went for a ride around the country on the dragon's back instead, and enjoyed it so much that he did not return home for three years.

In the meantime, his younger brother, who loved killing dragons, and hated croquet and dressing up, also went in search of the princess.

He spurred his horse across the hills and moorland, swam the width of the moat, chased away the green-eyed goggle and leapt up the steps of the tower three and four at a time.

And when he saw the princess, he threw her over his shoulder, carried her back to the palace and married her before she had time to argue.

So perhaps everything ended happily, after all.

The Kind Scarecrow

The farmer had put up a scarecrow to scare the crows away from his field of barley. He had made his body of sacking, stuffed with straw, and given him an old overcoat with brass buttons. The scarecrow's hair, too, was made of straw, which shone golden in the sunlight.

When the warm, spring breezes blew, the coat flapped wildly and the crows rose up in a great, black cloud. They flew off to the woods, making angry cawing noises. The green barley-shoots pushed further and further towards the sun and the scarecrow felt proud that he had protected them. But there were other birds in the field that he did not want to scare away.

The skylark sang so joyously, high up in the sky. The mottled thrush chirrupped and hopped around his feet in search of worms. But the scarecrow loved most of all the tiny bluetit. She would swing on his shoulder, calling out in a high, tinkling voice and chat with him.

One day the blackbird, who also sang sweetly, said to the scarecrow.

"I am building a nest of mud and straw, but there is so little straw about these days. The farmer has given you a fine thatch for your hair, scarecrow. Do you think you could spare me a little of it?"

"Of course. Take as much as you need," said the kind scarecrow.

He gave some to the blackbird and some to the skylark and some to the thrush. Soon he was quite bald.

Then he had a visit from magpie, who was bigger than the other birds. Magpie settled on scarecrow's arm and flicked his long, glossy, blue-green tail. He stared greedily at the coat-buttons.

"How they shine," said magpie, in his harsh, chattering way. "I do so love bright, pretty things. I have a very superior home, scarecrow – dome-shaped, with a side entrance. It's quite the latest fashion. I was going to decorate with milk-bottle tops – but brass buttons!" He sighed loudly. "I would be the envy of the whole neighbourhood."

The scarecrow thought that he did not really need the coat-buttons and he let magpie peck off, and fly away with, every one of them. But now his coat would not stay fastened and he felt very foolish, with his head so bald and his coat hanging open. He wondered if the birds would laugh at him, but they were far too busy working away at their nests.

The skylark had built a nest in some grasses. The blackbird had found an oak tree and the thrush had settled in a hawthorn hedge. Only the bluetit was homeless.

"How I wish I had a little nest," she told scarecrow tearfully. "Of moss and wool and feathers. Even a letterbox would do. But there aren't any letterboxes out here in the middle of the barley-field."

The scarecrow felt inside the warm, deep pocket of his overcoat.

"My pocket would make a lovely nest," he whispered. "And I could watch over the eggs for you."

With a happy cry of "Tsee Tsee ch-ch-ch," the bluetit flew off in search of moss. She flew over the head of the farmer, who had come into the field to check his barley crop. He stopped in surprise before the scarecrow.

"We can't have you looking like that, my lad," he said. "With your coat all over the place. And what has happened to the straw I gave you for hair?"

He went to the farmhouse and found a length of twine and an old hat his wife had put out for the jumble sale. It was a rather fine hat, made of tweed and shaped like a large pork pie. It had a red hatband fastened round it.

The farmer tied the scarecrow's coat with the

twine and put the hat on his head to hide the baldness.

"You're a fine, country squire now," he said. "All it needs is a feather."

When the farmer had gone indoors for his tea, the birds gathered round the scarecrow to admire his hat.

"I heard what the farmer said," sang the skylark. "Here is one of my best, white feathers for your hat, Scarecrow."

She plucked a feather from her breast and tucked it inside the hatband.

The blackbird put a glossy black feather in the hatband, and the thrush a feather of mottled brown. They all felt rather ashamed of taking so much straw from the scarecrow. The bluetit, who had not taken any straw, still plucked out feathers of blue and primrose-yellow.

The magpie was about to fly away, but the thrush called sharply to him. "Surely you can spare a feather, magpie, in return for all those lovely brass buttons."

And soon the scarecrow had a shiny, blue-green tailfeather in his hat as well.

When the farmer went out into the field, weeks later, he was amazed to see the scarecrow's hat so gay with feathers of many colours. On the scare-crow's shoulder perched a proud bluetit and from the deep pocket of his coat came the cheep of tiny birds, newly hatched from their eggs.

"Well, bless my soul. I wanted you to scare the birds away, not make friends with them," said the farmer.

But he was a kind-hearted man and the barley was growing well, so he gave a chuckle and went to tell the story to his wife.

Tadpole's Dream

Have you heard the story about a tadpole who lived in a bucket? No one knew *how* he had come to live in a bucket – not even his mother, the big green frog.

"But you always had to be different from the others," she croaked, "even when you were just a nitty, gritty bit of frogspawn."

When not too busy catching flies, she would perch on the rim of the bucket and tell him fairy stories. Tadpole's favourite story was about a frog who met a princess.

The princess was bouncing her golden ball by a pond one day when it fell into the water. A frog, who was sitting on a nearby water-lily leaf, rescued the ball and followed the princess back to her father's palace. There he ate food from a golden plate and, at night, slept in the princess's bedroom.

She placed him on her silken pillow and – lo and behold – he turned into a handsome prince.

Tadpole never tired of this story. While his brothers and sisters wriggled in and out of the bulrushes and burrowed in the soft black mud of the pond, he swam round and round his bucket. He dreamed of the day when he would grow into a frog and meet a princess.

Meanwhile, the tadpoles in the pond were growing strong back legs and their tails were becoming shorter.

"I don't see any signs of your back legs, my son," said the big green frog, peering down at him. "If you don't grow legs you will never be able to hop out of your bucket and see the world."

The tadpole knew that he would have to reach the pond in order to meet a princess. He worked hard at growing his back legs, and then his front legs, and soon his tail disappeared altogether. He had become a small green frog!

It was an exciting moment for the little frog when he hopped from his bucket and first felt grass under his feet. He hopped into a brightly coloured flowerbed, buzzing with insects. Then he hopped across a hard, gravel road and found his brothers and sisters in the lily-pond. They had become little frogs, too, and were having great fun in the warm sunshine, diving deep into the cool, green waters of the pond.

"Come and jump in the mud," they called to him.

"Come and chase the water-beetles!"

But the little green frog just sat on a water-lily leaf and tried to look important.

Day after sunny day, the little frogs played in the lily-pond. When the weather changed and the rain came pitter-pattering down they played hide-and-seek amongst the raindrops. They even rode on the back of the great, glittering dragonfly. And still the little green frog sat on the water-lily leaf and waited for his princess.

And one day a girl did come to the lily-pond. She was not playing with a golden ball, but a striped rubber one. Instead of a crown of precious stones she wore a crown of buttercups and daisies. But the little frog knew she must be a princess because she had golden curls, and when she bounced her rubber ball it fell into the water.

As he was trying hard to push it out with his nose, she picked him up and said, "Would you like to come home with me, Sir Frog?"

"Indeed, I would be honoured, Your Majesty," said the little green frog, who had been rehearsing his speech for ages.

He was carried along the gravel path, not in a coach drawn by white horses, but in a basket between the handle-bars of a bicycle. The palace, too, was not as grand as he had hoped for. Instead of having marble steps and turrets it was small and made of stone, with just two chimneys.

"When am I going to eat off a golden plate?" asked the little frog, getting rather anxious. "When are you going to take me upstairs and put me on your silken pillow?"

"A frog on my pillow? Yuk!" said the princess, who was really a little girl called Susie Brown.

"I've brought you home to put in my aquarium."

She put the little frog on a pebble in a glass box half full of water, and went outside to play.

And there he would be until this day, amongst the snails and plastic water-weed, if the big green frog had not hopped through the living room window and rescued him.

"You always have to be different, don't you?" she scolded. "Hop back to the pond this minute and play with your brothers and sisters in the mud. Chase the water beetles. Tickle the stickle-back. Catch a few flies and forget all this romantic nonsense."

And so he did.

But at night, when the wind sighs softly in the bulrushes, a little green frog climbs onto a water-lily leaf, gazes at the moon, and dreams his dreams.

For even when he becomes a frog, and learns the way of the world, a tadpole's nature never really changes.

The Rainbow Pearl

A fishergirl lived in a hut at the edge of the ocean. Mountains rose up high above the ocean, and the waters turned from blue in the shallow parts to deep, mysterious green.

On hot, stifling days, when there was scarcely even a sea breeze blowing, the girl would tie up her hair in a cotton scarf, wade into the water, swim a little way, and then dive down to the sandy bed in the shallow part of the ocean, where the oysters lived.

The oysters were her friends. For them, she would clear away the broken nets and straggling seaweed and chase away the crabs and lobsters and hungry fish which might harm them.

In return, the oysters would open up their shells and swallow small pebbles from the ocean bed. For days, months, years even, they would build upon the tiny pebbles layer upon layer of a shining substance. And, slowly but surely, beautiful round pearls would be formed.

As each pearl became ready, the fishergirl would take it gently from the mouth of the oyster. The pearls were in great demand by princesses and prime ministers for crowns, diadems and necklaces. But the fishergirl took them sparingly, for she did not wish for great wealth. She was happy in her hut by the ocean, although perhaps she felt a little lonely sometimes.

One hot day, when the sun had blistered her arms and the white sand burned her feet, the fishergirl spent longer than usual diving into the cool green waters of the ocean. She had learnt to hold her breath for a long time and could enjoy, as she worked, the sight of tiny, coloured fishes, bright as jewels, which darted in and out of the seaferns and banks of star-shaped coral.

But suddenly she heard a tiny sobbing sound coming from where the ferns grew thickest. Pushing them aside with a stick she saw a baby oyster, half buried in the sand, and hopelessly entwined with bladders of dark brown seaweed.

The fishergirl worked away at the sand with her stick and carefully pulled the seaweed from the fan-shaped shell of the baby oyster. The baby oyster stopped crying at once and opened his shell a little in a sort of grin.

"Now don't do that," said the fishergirl kindly, "or you will have all sorts of pebbles and bits of things in your mouth before you know it. You're only a baby oyster, and not ready for making pearls yet."

And she gently lifted the baby oyster and put him on a part of the ocean bed where the water ran clear and sparkling, and where he could chat to the little coloured fishes, and play hide and seek with them.

After that, every day, when her work on the seabed was done, the fishergirl went to make sure that the baby oyster was safe, and growing properly.

One day, she saw a huge crab with bulbous eyes on stalks and wicked pincers moving sideways, in the way that crabs do, towards the baby oyster.

"There's a tasty morsel inside that shell!" chuckled the crab. "And I'll nip it open in no time."

He waved his pincers in the air. The fishergirl was beside the baby oyster in a moment.

"If you don't go away and stay away," she shouted, "I'll have those claws of yours for clothes-pegs. They're just what I need for a windy Monday morning."

The crab turned and scuttled away as fast as he could, and was never seen again.

Another day, a big, black fish, with flashing eyes and rows of teeth on the outside of his body, came gliding towards the baby oyster.

"I've swum all the way from the deepest part of

the ocean," boomed the fish. "In the deepest part of the ocean it's always as black as night. There is nothing much to eat down there and I'm very hungry."

"I'm hungry too," shouted the fishergirl. "And my favourite food is big black fish on toast."

And the fish swam hurriedly back to the deepest part of the ocean.

At night, in her little hut, the fishergirl often thought of the baby oyster and hoped he was asleep and safe in his home on the ocean bed.

But one night a big black cloud covered the moon and the wind began to howl like a thousand demons. The fishergirl could hear the waves hammering the shoreline. She felt sickness in her stomach and a chill in her bones. She pulled on a warm cloak and rushed downstairs, out of her hut, and across the dark sands, heavy with water.

Through the many voices which that night possessed the wind, the fishergirl heard the faint cry of the baby oyster. The strong waves had torn him from his bed at the bottom of the ocean, and were carrying him out to the open sea.

Throwing off her cloak, the fishergirl plunged into the ocean. Choking and blinded, she crashed through waves, spat out foam, struggled and kicked and reached the baby oyster. She swam back to the shore with him and they sat together, looking out to sea, until the wind died down, and the waves grew calm, and the early morning sun came out.

And, as sometimes happens when the last drops of rain meet the first glimmer of sunshine, a rainbow arched its beautiful colours of red, blue, gold and indigo across the sands and into the ocean.

When the fishergirl pointed out the rainbow, the baby oyster opened his shell in wonder. And when he closed it again, inside his shell was a tiny piece of the rainbow.

"I really don't like to put you back into the ocean," the fishergirl said. "It is so dangerous there. Perhaps you should come with me to my hut. I could make a pond in the garden and put some seawater in it."

The baby oyster knew he would miss all his friends at the bottom of the ocean, but he loved the fishergirl more than anyone in the world.

"I love you more than anyone in the world," he told her. "But I must go back to the ocean. I have work to do there."

He felt very excited about the bit of rainbow inside his shell. But he knew he could not tell the fishergirl about it.

So the baby oyster, who by now had grown into quite a big oyster, went back to his home in the ocean. Every day the fishergirl went to see that all was well, and every day he worked secretly on the piece of rainbow inside him, building upon it layer after layer of beautiful shining pearl.

Months passed, years passed. The fishergirl grew older, but the oyster grew older still, for not all sea-creatures last as long as humans do. And one day when the fishergirl visited him the oyster said, "I am getting old and tired, and I would like to sleep a long sleep. But before I do, take the gift I have been working on all these years. It is ready now."

The fishergirl gently opened the oyster's shell, and cried out in amazement at the wondrous pearl which lay there, glowing with all the beautiful colours of the rainbow. She lifted it from the oyster's shell. Then she kissed him tenderly and covered him with the softest fern and whitest flowers of the sea.

In the years that followed, many rich and famous people asked to buy the rainbow pearl from the fishergirl, but never would she part with it. She wore it always on a silver chain, close to her heart, and it cheered her days and made even the dark nights a little brighter.

The Fat Princess

This is a story about a rather fat princess.

She was very pretty and very cuddly, but she found it difficult to squeeze into her dresses when getting ready for balls and banquets – and then she would start to be cross with her lady-in-waiting. It was not the lady-in-waiting's fault that zips would not zip and buttons would not button, and the princess knew this. But at the banquets and royal feasts, matters went from bad to worse.

The princess, you see, simply could not resist cream cakes, puddings and pastries. Although visiting princes and prime ministers were content with one cream cake, the princess had to have four, or five, and then a helping of jelly and ice cream and a plate of chocolate biscuits.

At one such feast, when the princess was tucking into a large dish of toffee trifle, someone tapped her shoulder and made her jump in a rather guilty way. She turned to see a frail old lady, with gold-rimmed spectacles, and wings sprouting out of the shoulders of her party dress.

"You won't remember me," said the old lady. "You were a baby when I saw you last – and quite chubby, even then. I am your fairy godmother. I can see that you have a problem and I am going to help you with it."

She muttered some rather nasty-sounding words, touched the princess with a silver wand that had a tarnished star on top, and flew out of the window.

"What does she mean by saying I have a problem?" muttered the princess. "Just because I'm a bit on the plump side."

There was a sound of tearing material as she reached out for a large meringue – and then a strange thing happened. The sugary meringue, as soon as she took hold of it, turned into a white and green cauliflower.

The princess looked in amazement at the cauliflower and put it back on the banqueting table. She picked up a brandy-snap and it turned into a large carrot.

"That horrid old woman!" cried the princess. She threw down the carrot, stamped her foot and burst into tears.

Try as she might, the princess could get nothing that she wanted to eat at the banquet. Every time she picked up a cake or a pastry it turned into a vegetable or a piece of fruit. The spell did not only last the evening of the banquet, either. It went on and on, until the princess became quite slim and sylph-like. But she was not as pretty and cuddly as before, because whenever she saw a stick of rhubarb or a spring onion her face took on a terrible scowl.

She asked the lady-in-waiting for help, but the lady-in-waiting was so glad to zip zips and button buttons without being shouted at, she pretended not to know what was bothering the princess.

She asked the cook for help, but the cook was so tired of whipping bowls of cream until her arm ached, only to see them turn into bowls of horse-radish sauce as soon as the princess touched them, that she nearly threw the lot in her direction.

But there was one person who did want to help the princess, because he was secretly in love with her, and that was the gardener's boy. The gardener's boy was the seventh son of a seventh son, and very intelligent. And, one day, when he came upon the princess weeping in the royal rose garden, he took off his cap, approached her timidly and said, "Your Highness, I have heard about your royal predicament and think I may have found a way out of it. I understand the problem began with a meringue which turned into a cauliflower. Perhaps you would allow me to escort you to a cauliflower patch I have been tending."

"Cauliflower patch!" cried the princess. "What do

I want with a cauliflower patch? I never wish to see another cauliflower for as long as I live."

But she followed the gardener's boy, just the same, because he was already out of earshot and on his way to the royal allotment.

"What you need to do," explained the boy, when the princess caught up with him "is to reverse your fairy godmother's spell by standing on your head."

The princess opened her mouth to call the guards to throw the gardener's boy into jail for making such a suggestion. But then she saw his blue eyes twinkling at her, and thought it might be rather fun to try standing on her head. And, because she was now so slim, she found standing on her head very easy.

When she was nicely upside down, and had stopped wobbling, the gardener's boy dug up a cauliflower, washed it under the garden hose, and handed it to the princess. As she took it, the cauliflower turned into a big, sugary meringue, with lashings of cream, and chocolate flakes on top. The princess gave a cry of joy and stood on her feet again. But, as soon as she did so, the meringue turned back into a cauliflower.

"You will have to practise eating upside down," said the gardener's boy. "It's quite easy when you get the hang of it."

And, to make the princess feel better, he stood on his head as well.

The princess was so grateful to the gardener's boy

that she asked him to marry her and, as he was the seventh son of a seventh son, he was made a duke immediately and put in charge of the Royal Garden Mint.

At the wedding feast there was one long table laid for guests, crammed with cakes, sweets and pastries and one for the princess laden with vegetables and fruit.

Sometimes the princess stayed the right way up and nibbled at half a grapefruit, or a lettuce leaf, or a piece of celery and sometimes she stood on her head and the celery became icing sugar and the grapefruit a steamed pudding with treacle on top.

But, because of all the exercise involved, she was just the same shape at the end of the banquet as at the beginning of it, and went off for her honeymoon in a hot air balloon.

I think I saw it the other day. It had a large tomato painted on one side and a cream bun on the other.

The princess and the gardener's boy were standing in a basket, waving their arms about. They looked happy as can be.

Jinny Greenteeth

On her way home from school, Verity passed the water-wheel. It had once been used to work the mill, but now the wheel was out of action and its blades had grown rusty and brown.

The waters of the mill-pond, too, were still and silent. Water-buttercups and thick green scum covered the surface of the pond and the ducks and moorhens would not go near it. They splashed and squawked further down the river.

"Stay away from the mill-pond," warned Verity's mother. "Or Jinny Greenteeth will get you."

She said this because the waters of the mill-pond were deep, and dangerous to children. But her own mother had warned *her* about Jinny Greenteeth and she still half believed in the old witch. For it was said that Jinny Greenteeth lived just under the water-buttercups, and that if a child so much as dabbled its fingers in the water she would drag that child down under the bright green scum.

After school, Verity would dawdle near the mill-pond, half-hoping, half-dreading, to see Jinny Greenteeth. She did not climb down to the water's edge, of course – she was not brave, or foolhardy enough for that. But she would stare down at the water, edged with bulrushes and popping with water-beetles, and try to catch a glimpse of long, green witch's hair.

There was a funny smell about the water. It smelt the way flower stems do when they have been left in a vase for a long time. "Does Jinny Greenteeth have that sort of smell," thought Verity? "She would be very old, and her hair would be long and slimy, like water weed."

There was a sudden movement in the water, and under the scummy surface a dark shadow moved. Verity screamed and ran.

The next day, Saturday, was warm and sunny. The bright sun shone everywhere except on the waters of the mill-pond. Verity, on a shopping errand for her mother, was surprised to see a girl of her own age right down at the water's edge, trying to pick the water-buttercups.

"Don't do that!" Verity called. "It's dangerous."

The girl made signs that she could not hear her, and beckoned to Verity. Verity climbed down to the level of the mill-pond, but she kept well away from the water.

"It's dangerous," she shouted, but the girl shook her head and again leaned over the water. She cupped her hands over something, and held it towards Verity.

"Look what I got."

Her voice was soft and murmuring, like the sounds of streams under the hillside.

"I got treasure here."

"Treasure?" said Verity, moving a little nearer "What sort of treasure?"

"Rainbow gossamer," said the girl. "I got rainbow gossamer and emeralds here."

She gazed at Verity and her eyes turned from blue to green, like moving water.

"You don't believe me? Look then. Come over here and look."

As Verity moved towards her, the girl opened out her hands and up into the air flew a dragonfly, with wings of gossamer and a body the colour of flashing jewels. The girl reached towards Verity and took hold of her hand. Her long white fingers were cold and damp and she wore a silver ring with a large, round stone set into it.

"See him fly," she whispered, pointing up at the dragonfly and Verity saw, as if in a dream, the soft whiteness of her skin and the silvery glint of her long, flowing hair.

"Is she a girl my age?" wondered Verity. "Or is she much, much older?"

"Oh," said the girl, as if reading her thoughts. "I'm much, much older. I'm as old as the hills, as old as the streams, as old as the gems in the deep dark caverns. You know my name, don't you, Verity? You know what I'm called."

And then she smiled, very slowly, showing teeth as green and scummy as the water. Verity pulled and pulled so hard that the long white arm of Jinny Greenteeth elongated like an octopus and she sank with a sigh and the merest ripple beneath the surface of the mill-pond.

Verity ran away as fast as she could, and it was not until she was safely home that she found she was holding the silver ring with the big round stone in it. She hid it under her mattress and for days was afraid to look at it.

But when she did, she saw the stone turn from blue to green like moving water and a sound of murmuring came from the stone, the way the sound of waves can be heard in a sea-shell.

And although she always meant to throw the ring back into the mill-pond, she dreaded the thought of a long, white octopus arm coming up to claim it. And so she kept the ring, and marvelled at it even when she was quite an old lady.

The Kingdom Under the Hill

There was once a boy called Peter who liked stories of witches, dragons and princesses, as many children do. But most of all he loved the stories his grandfather told him of the Kingdom Under the Hill.

The hill rose up just behind the village where Peter lived, and to the passer-by it looked like any other hill. Bees whirred amongst the clover and wild primroses peeped from its grassy slopes.

"But underneath," said his grandfather, "underneath it is a magic place."

And he told Peter wondrous tales, of huge caverns lined with glittering quartz and of tiny men who mined gold – a gold as fine and strong and precious as the hair of the woman who lived in a palace in the Kingdom Under the Hill. The woman, said Peter's grandfather, was as white and cold as marble and when the dwarves had mined the gold, others fashioned it on silver anvils into rich and beautiful treasures for her.

"If you stand on the hill when the wind has dropped and there is no sound," he told Peter, "whether it be day or night, you will hear the tap-tapping of the hammers on the silver anvils."

Many times Peter climbed the hill and put his ear to the soft grass and trembling earth, and once he heard a faint tap-tapping sound.

Peter grew in height and strength, took a job and found himself a sweetheart, but still he remembered the tales his grandfather had told him of the Kingdom Under the Hill. And once, when walking with his sweetheart on the brow of the hill, he thought he heard the tapping noise again.

"What tapping?" said the girl. "I hear no tapping."

And because the sky was blue and the birds were singing, she bent and picked a tiny blue flower from the hillside, kissed it, and gave it to Peter with her love.

The next morning Peter took a spade to the hillside and began shovelling earth from the side of it. But though he worked until his arms ached and his knees ached, he could find no way into the hard brown earth.

In the afternoon he hired a great orange machine from a nearby farm and drove it, clanking, towards the hillside. But the people from his village shouted and chased after him, shaking their fists.

"You let the hillside be," they cried. "It's not your hillside. And we like it the way it is."

As they knew nothing of the Kingdom Under the Hill, they saw the yellow prickly gorse, the tiny hillocks where the rabbits played, and were content with it.

That night, when walking on the hilltop, Peter found a four-leaf clover – and at that moment the direction of the wind changed. Peter stepped into a disused mineshaft which opened up in front of him, and fell down, down, down, into the darkness of the Kingdom Under the Hill.

He must have banged his head and lain unconscious for several hours. When he opened his eyes it was to find himself in the glittering cavern his grandfather had told him of so many years before.

Small brown wizened men were peering at him with lanterns, and jumping about excitedly. They poked at him with gnarled fingers and chattered in a language Peter could not understand. The walls of the cavern shone purple in the lantern-lights, and the lights reflected themselves in heaps of glowing gold.

One of the little men whistled, and together they pushed and pulled until Peter was on his feet, with his head almost touching the roof of the cavern. The man whistled again, and beckoned, and Peter followed him into a room full of dwarves working away at silver anvils. Beyond that he entered a high-ceilinged cavern, dripping with stalactites like pointed candles, where piles of crowns and cups and shields and other golden treasures lay.

He followed the little man for what seemed like miles, over floors green and slippery with moss, and through silver corridors and caverns of rose-quartz and snow crystal.

Then, suddenly, the caverns opened out into a wide courtyard with crystal pools and marble fountains and, at the head of the courtyard, on a silver throne, he saw the woman white as marble, with hair as fine as gold.

As she rose and moved towards him, Peter saw that the woman's eyes were green as emeralds, and as cold and hard as emeralds too. But, when she put her white hand on his shoulder, he forgot the hardness of her eyes and saw only how beautiful they were.

"I have been waiting for a long, long time," said the woman of marble. She took Peter through her shining palace and into her gardens, where the roses were made of jewels and the leaves of the rose-trees silver and copper. And the white doves which sat on the marble dovecote were silent and still.

"In the daytime you will tend my garden," said

the woman. "And at night you will sleep in my bed."

And all day Peter tended the jewelled flowers, and at night he slept in the bed of the woman of marble, and gazed up at the ceiling which opened out into a sky of dark blue velvet, where stars glittered like small hard diamonds and the moon of marble reflected the face of the woman of marble who lay beside him. And so, many months passed.

And then, one day, when polishing the silver and copper leaves of the rose-tree, Peter saw at his feet a tiny flower with a head made up of five small sparkling blue stones. As he picked the flower, and held it close to his heart, something stirred in his memory and hot tears began to flow down his cheeks, now pale from lack of sun. As the tears fell onto the flower, the five blue stones turned to blue petals, and the stiff metal stem in Peter's fingers relaxed and gave out fresh green leaves.

Through his tears, Peter saw the woman of marble standing before him, but her bright green eyes were fading into blue and her cheeks were becoming round and rosy. He found himself standing with his sweetheart on the brow of the hill again, with the sky blue and the birds singing, and the tiny blue flower still clutched in his hand.

Peter never tried to return to the Kingdom Under the Hill. He built a cottage for himself and his sweetheart and in the garden they grew flowers –

red roses, blue forget-me-nots, purple columbines and yellow pansies.

And, unlike the flowers in the jewelled garden, they wafted sweet scents on the summer breeze, welcomed the bees to their hearts, kissed the butterflies, had their day and died.

The Boggart and the Bakewell Pudding

This is a story of a boggart and some strange happenings at an inn which can be found in the town of Bakewell, Derbyshire.

Now a boggart, in case you have never seen one, is a sort of goblin with long, lanky legs and long, lanky arms. Boggarts are naughty, mischievous creatures and in the daytime they can make themselves invisible, so it is easy for them to play tricks on people.

This particular boggart lived in the kitchen of the inn. He liked living in the kitchen because it gave him the chance to get up to all sorts of mischief. And when the little kitchen-maid knelt to clean the kitchen-range, dipping her brush into a tin of lead-polish (as kitchen-maids did in the old days) what would the boggart do but dip his long, bony fingers in the lead-polish and smear the whitewashed walls with it. Then one day he stretched out his long, bony arm to where a joint of meat was roasting on a spit in front of the fire, gave it a flick of his wrist, and round and round spun the joint of meat, splashing gravy everywhere.

When she saw the mess of lead-polish on the walls and rich brown gravy flying in all directions, the cook in charge of the kitchen became very cross with the kitchen-maid, and the kitchen-maid was so upset that she could not sleep that night and tiptoed downstairs to the kitchen to pour herself a glass of water.

This was before the days of electricity and the kitchen-maid had to light her way with a candle. The candle flame threw such ghostly shadows across the kitchen that when she heard a sudden rustling sound in the corner the kitchen-maid nearly jumped out of her skin. And when she looked towards the corner, what she saw made her scream out loud. For the round, wicked eyes of the boggart, shining yellow in the moonlight, were watching her from the face of the grandfather clock!

After that, the kitchen-maid would never go into the kitchen at night. The Irish boy who cleaned the silver said that he was not afraid of boggarts, and that if the boggart did not stop playing tricks on the kitchen-maid he would play a few tricks on *him*.

But the cook in charge of the kitchen had read

somewhere that what boggarts love most is a dish of cream, freshly churned and thick and frothy. And so every night she made it her business to put out cream for the boggart in a blue earthenware dish with a pattern of white flowers on it. And the cream pleased the boggart so much that he stopped tormenting the kitchen-maid and at night performed tricks that were more high spirits than naughtiness – like swinging on the fly-catcher and taking the lid off the tall stone bread-crock and diving into it.

But one night the cook in charge of the kitchen forgot to leave the dish of cream out for the boggart. She had a lot on her mind, because the next day, at twelve, a party from a nearby manor-house would be coming for a feast at the inn. And the cook was so busy thinking about the big, fat goose she was going to roast, and the strawberry tart she was going to bake, that she quite forgot the boggart. The thirsty boggart sulked inside his clock the whole night long. And in the morning he was ripe and ready for mischief.

All this happened a long time ago, when your great-great- great- great-grandparents were alive. And, as you know, in those days rich people dressed in silks and satins and wore hats with feathers and drove around in grand carriages drawn by dappled horses. But when one such carriage drew up by the steps at the front of the inn, the cook in the kitchen at the back was having a terrible time.

For the naughty boggart had spun the goose round and round so fast on its spit in front of the kitchen fire, that it had flown across the kitchen as if come to life again. He had emptied so much pepper into the soup that the cook could not stop sneezing. And when she tried to make the pastry for the strawberry tart he sat, all invisible, on the weighing scales so that she could not measure the butter properly. He played marbles with the eggs, and shook and shook the flour-sprinkler so that if it had not been summer you would have thought that the roof of the kitchen had blown away and the snow was blizzarding in.

From time to time the cook had a little drink from a glass bottle on the dresser – to prevent her from breaking down and bursting into tears, you understand – and so she managed to stop some of the eggs from rolling off the table, and broke them into a basin and beat them to a froth with an egg-beater that all the time was twitching and turning and trying to leap out of her hand. And then she went to the larder to find a pot of strawberry jam.

But the boggart had already had his fingers in the strawberry jam and the sticky mess was running down his arms as far as the elbow joints. When he had licked his fingers clean he took a long drink from the glass bottle on the dresser, and when the cook's back was turned he tipped the contents of the bottle into the egg mixture. He ran round and round in circles grabbing at all the jars and bottles he could find – great big pot ones, little squat ones, silver-topped ones and plop- plop- plop-he emptied them all into the mixing bowl. Then he plunged his long arms into the mixture, right up to the armpits, and stirred in such a frenzy that it went flying everywhere.

When the poor cook saw what was happening she gave a cry of rage. The visitors in the next room had finished their goose and were rattling their spoons and forks. In her panic, the cook poured the mixture on top of the jam, instead of into the pastry, and pushed it all into the oven, just as it was.

But what do you think – when the pudding was served up at table, all golden and bubbly, the company were delighted. And when they had eaten it, they said it was the best pudding they had ever tasted. They said they would tell all their friends about it and that soon the pudding would be famous throughout Bakewell and the rest of Derbyshire.

Now the boggart had been listening to all this at the door of the dining-room and his head became quite swollen up with pride. And while the cook was talking to the guests he dashed straight back to the kitchen to try to invent another famous pudding. But this time he poured black treacle into a large stone bowl, and when he plunged his arms in, up to the armpits, there they stuck. The cook, on her return, was so pink and flushed from the success of the Bakewell Pudding that she cleared up the kitchen rather hastily. She did not notice the bowl of treacle or, of course, the boggart, who was still invisible.

In fact no one knew anything about the boggart until the middle of the night, when a terrible cursing and howling echoed through all the rooms of the inn.

The cook and the kitchen-maid and the boy who cleaned the silver rushed into the kitchen in their night-gowns – and for the first time they saw the tall, lanky boggart with his ugly, round face and beady eyes, stuck up to his armpits in thick, black treacle.

When he saw their angry faces, the boggart pulled and tugged, and tugged and pulled until his arms came out of the pudding basin all shiny and black. He shot out of the kitchen, along the corridor, and out of the door of the inn. But, as he did so, his arms became stuck on the inn walls, and though he tugged and pulled, and pulled again, and said many rude words in boggart language, there they stayed – for the treacle had hardened and stuck fast.

With the coming of dawn, the face and body of the boggart became invisible, but his hands and arms, covered in black teacle, were there for all to see.

Nowadays, people from all over the world have heard of the Bakewell Pudding. The inn is a hotel called the Rutland Arms, and a fine hotel it is too. And if you go to the centre of Bakewell, and climb the hotel steps, you will see the boggart's arms – as long and black and ugly as ever.

You will not see the boggart, of course, in the daytime. But if you go on a dark, spooky night, when the wind is howling, you might just see the shape of a goblin body, and wicked goblin eyes gleaming yellow in the moonlight as they did, all those years ago, inside the grandfather clock.

And if the arms on the hotel wall shake a little, people who have not heard this story will say it is vibration from the traffic on Rutland Square. But we know better, don't we? We know it is the boggart tugging and pulling, pulling and tugging, trying to escape as he has for a hundred years and more.

Poor old boggart. I feel a bit sorry for him – don't you?

The Princess who met the North Wind

There was once a princess who lived in a very cold land. The white mountains reached almost to the sky, and the rivers shone silver as the chain the princess wore around her neck.

The king and queen loved their daughter very much and gave her beautiful presents each birthday, but the time came when she had far too much of everything.

"Not another ruby snow-bird's egg!" said the princess crossly, as she opened up her parcels. "I have three already." "Take away these pearls – I have enough to play marbles with."

"But my child, what *can* we give you?" asked the poor king, wringing his hands. "I've searched high and low to find you something different this year."

"I think," said the princess, "that until you can give me the most beautiful jewels in the world to hang on my necklace, I will forget about birthdays."

And she stamped up to bed, taking no notice of her cake, which was built in the shape of an iceberg. The king shook his head sadly, and gave the pearls to the youngest parlourmaid.

That night, as the princess lay sleeping, the north wind began to call and blow around her room at the top of the palace. He blew so fiercely that the heavy clouds rolled away across the sky and the stars shone, clear and bright, into the bedroom. The princess thought it must be daylight and sat up in bed, staring and blinking.

"Come to the window, Princess," sang the north wind, "and I will give you the most beautiful jewels in the world for your necklace."

The princess ran to the window and looked up at the sky, where thousands of stars were twinkling and glistening.

"Oh, how beautiful," she whispered. "If only I could reach them."

"Put on your cloak and shoes and come with me, Princess," said the north wind. And he led her down the stairs, through the palace gates, and up the side of the highest mountain in the kingdom.

The princess was not at all happy on the mountain. Her feet were wet, her hands numb, and all the time the north wind blew so hard that her cloak billowed and swelled. The more she climbed, the further away the stars seemed to be, twinkling and laughing.

"They are so beautiful," she gasped to the north wind, "but there must be an easier way to reach them."

"Look down, look down," sang the north wind. And the princess stared in surprise, for now the stars were below as well as above her, and the whole night seemed on fire with them.

"I must have the stars for my necklace!" she cried, and began to slide and slither down the mountain, tearing her cloak, and cutting her hands on the rocks.

The princess did not realize that the cold breath of the north wind had frozen the lake below the mountain, and that all she could see was the reflection of the stars from the sky above. She reached the bottom of the mountain, ran to the lake, stretched out her hand for the nearest star, and gave a cry of bitter disappointment.

The north wind blew so hard that the pine trees shivered and the snow fell from their branches onto the princess. She tried to pull her cloak together, but it was badly torn.

"How silly I have been," said the princess, "to think I could capture the stars. And here I am at the bottom of a mountain, frozen and hungry, and miles from home."

As the princess thought of her warm bed, and the birthday tea she had refused to eat, and the kindness of her mother and father, three tears trickled down her nose and chin and hung, frozen, to her silver necklace.

Suddenly the branches of the pine trees stopped shivering, and all was still. A young man appeared at the side of the princess and pointed to the frozen tears which clung to her necklace, gleaming green, purple and blue in the Northern Lights.

"I am the Prince of the North Wind," he said, "and I have given you the most beautiful jewels in the world."

He took the princess by the hand and led her back to the palace, where there was much laughter and rejoicing.

The Woman who grew Butterflies

In the little town of Bunting stood a neat row of cottages. The cottage steps were always freshly washed, and the doors were brightly painted in all the colours of the rainbow.

"There never was a row as pretty as ours," said Mrs Gordon, who lived in the first cottage.

"And our gardens are a sight for sore eyes," said Mr Bennett, who lived in the second cottage.

"All except for one," sighed Mr and Mrs Bunce, who lived in the third cottage. "And that's not a sight for sore eyes, it's nothing but an eyesore."

And they pointed to the fourth cottage, where Old Molly lived.

Old Molly, you see, was very kind to animals. And not just animals, either. She fed the birds with bread and nuts and grain in the winter months. And in the summer she would not tread on a snail or slug if she could help it.

Her neighbours would not allow snails and slugs in their gardens. And more than anything they hated caterpillars. They went to the gardening shop and bought spray guns and puffer bottles which kill at the touch of a button. So all the snails and slugs and caterpillars made their way to Old Molly's garden. She had not the heart to harm them, and soon they had eaten everything in sight!

"That silly woman hasn't a single flower left," sniffed Mrs Gordon, as she tended her roses.

"And look at her apple tree. Not a leaf on it," sneered Mr Bennett, as he trimmed his hedge.

"She won't stand a chance in the competition," sniggered Mr and Mrs Bunce. "What the Mayor will say we can't imagine."

For in a week's time the Mayor of Bunting was to choose the most beautiful garden and present the owner with a big, silver cup.

"I will fill it with roses from my garden," thought Mrs Gordon, as she polished her sideboard.

"I will put it in the window, where everyone can see it," thought Mr Bennett, as he trimmed his hedge another few inches.

"I will have it on my side of the bed one week," said Mr Bunce.

"And I will have it on my side the other," agreed his wife.

Old Molly was not thinking of roses or hedgerows or silver cups. She was looking at the caterpillars in her garden, which had grown so fat they had stopped eating and wrapped themselves up in bundles.

"You'll soon be bursting out of your skins," she chuckled. "And then what little beauties you will be."

Seven days later the Mayor of Bunting arrived. He drove the car himself, and the bonnet of his car was painted to look like a large bumblebee. His waistcoat was embroidered with bluebottles, and from his ear dangled an earring shaped like a golden ant.

First he looked at Mrs Gordon's garden, at her lawn as neat as a pocket-handkerchief, her spiky trellis-work and roses.

"Ten marks out of fifty for trying," said the Mayor.

Then he looked at Mr Bennett's garden, his well-trimmed hedge, his well-tended patio and his garden-gnomes.

"Five out of fifty," said the Mayor, who did not like garden-gnomes.

He was about to give Mr and Mrs Bunce eight points each for their lily-pond when his eye was attracted to Old Molly's garden.

For in the night the butterflies had climbed out of their hard little caterpillar-jackets and they were clinging to all the branches of the appletree. They quivered and gleamed in the sunlight like thousands of blossoms – orange, flame-red, lavender and mauve.

The slugs and snails had been busy in the night, too, and the yard outside Old Molly's house was patterned in shining silver. On the roof white fluffy doves, rosy finches and tiny bluetits preened themselves and twittered and cooed.

"What a magnificent sight!" cried the Mayor, rubbing the bluebottles on his waistcoat.

"Two-hundred out of fifty, without any doubt."

Then he gave Old Molly the big silver cup and drove home, humming an opera tune, for egg on toast, honey sandwiches and rose-hip tea.

Old Molly stared at the cup. She saw the reflection of her wizened brown face and giggled. Then she put the cup on her mantelpiece and it stayed there for the rest of the summer, and throughout the winter, too.

But with the coming of spring, Old Molly was too busy to clean silver. So she put the cup in the garden, and a robin built her nest in it.

The Hagge Tree

Lucy did not like her cousin Arnold. He was always telling her bad, nasty things. He did not tell her these things in front of grown-ups. But now Lucy's mother, who wanted to talk to Arnold's mother, had sent them to play in Lucy's bedroom.

"What a horrible tree," said Arnold. He stared out of the bedroom window at a tree which grew at the far end of the garden. "That's a Hagge Tree." He kicked the leg of Lucy's chair. "Don't you want to know what a Hagge Tree is?"

Lucy did not want to know.

"A Hagge Tree," said Arnold, "is really a witch in disguise. Can't you see that face in the trunk? And those branches aren't really branches. They're knotted hair."

Lucy looked at the tree. She saw a witch-like

shape with a humped back and long, straggling hair and shivered.

"If you tear a branch from the Hagge Tree," said Arnold, "it shrieks and bleeds. Real blood."

"I don't believe you," said Lucy. "Why would a witch want to be a tree? Witches like to ride on broomsticks and put spells on people."

"They sometimes put spells on themselves," replied Arnold. "She turns back into a witch at midnight. You'll see."

That night Lucy looked fearfully out of her bedroom window. In the half-light the tree looked more like a witch than ever. Lucy shivered again and drew the curtains right across the window. She took her teddybear to bed with her – a thing she had not done for years. And when a voice woke her in the dead of night she knew at once who it was.

The old witch was actually sitting on Lucy's bedpost! She had long, matted hair and a big chin and a wart on the end of her nose. There was a nasty smell about her too.

"Rotting wood," thought Lucy, feeling rather sick.

The witch opened her mouth and grinned. Her teeth were like broken tombstones.

"If you would be rid of me
Tear a branch from the Hagge Tree."

cackled the witch. And then she was gone, leaving a trail of rotting leaves behind her.

The next night Lucy asked if she could sleep in her mother and father's bedroom. They told her not to be silly, but her mother sat and read her a bedtime story until she fell asleep.

And then, at dead of night, the witch appeared again. She wagged a finger like a gnarled old twig at Lucy and pointed to the window. Then she said, in a loud rasping voice,

"The moon is frowning,
Bats flit black,
Pull and twist and shake and hack."

"No!" cried Lucy, gathering the bedclothes tightly round herself. "No, I won't!"

"You must," croaked the witch, and then she sang, in a voice as ghastly as a corn-crake,

"You never will be rid of me
If you don't tear a branch from the
Hagge Tree."

On the third night Lucy slept soundly. The witch had to poke her with long, bony fingers to wake her up.

"Go away," muttered Lucy. She was so tired, she hardly cared if the witch sat on her bedpost or not.

The witch rolled eyes like green poached eggs at her. Then she started chanting.

"Gaze at the moon till it hurts your eyes.
Fight through cobwebs thick with flies.
Though screech-owl swoops to peck your nose,
Though worms of darkness nibble your
toes . . ."

"Stop it! Stop it!" cried Lucy, holding her pillow to her ears "Don't go on and on. I know what's coming. And I *will* tear a branch from the stupid Hagge Tree if it will stop you cackling and waking me up every night."

The witch looked rather offended. Then she said sulkily, "You'd never dare anyway. Remember what Arnold said." And she disappeared in a puff of bonfire smoke.

Lucy climbed out of bed and drew back the curtains. The witch had already reached the bottom of the garden and turned back into a wicked-looking tree again. In the moonlight, the face in the trunk seemed to be smirking at Lucy. Lucy pulled on her dressing-gown and went downstairs.

She stepped outside into a jungle of strange shadows. The moon was half hidden by cloud. All around she heard the rustling and whispering of a thousand creepy-crawly things.

"Why, it's Lucy . . . Hello, Lucy. We've been waiting for you, Lucy."

The trees and bushes in the garden were shrouded with thick cobwebs. Above her head an owl screeched and flapped its wings and a tiny mouse squealed somewhere in the undergrowth.

And then the moon turned silver and sailed out from behind the clouds. The garden was bathed in a silver light. A spider dropped by Lucy's head and said, in a tinkling voice, "Don't break my web, Lucy. I spent so many hours spinning it."

Lucy promised that she would not. And as she walked across the grass, wet with silver dew, a little worm popped up its head and said, "Be careful how you go, Lucy. Don't tread on us with your big, flat feet."

So Lucy tiptoed carefully, all the way down the garden, to the Hagge Tree.

When she reached the Hagge Tree, Lucy was surprised that she did not feel very frightened after all. Looking up at the dark, humped shape she thought of what Arnold had said.

"If you tear a branch from the Hagge Tree it shrieks and bleeds. Real blood."

She thought of the old witch shouting. "Pull and twist and shake and hack," in her rasping voice.

But the tree hung its branches wearily in the moonlight and the face in the trunk looked wizened and sad.

Lucy stood on her toes, closed her eyes, and gently touched one black branch of the Hagge Tree. It crumbled into her hand with a pitiful little sigh. Then she took the branch back to her bedroom and stood it in a jar of water.

* * *

When Lucy awoke next morning, the sun was shining and her room was full of a strange and wonderful perfume. The branch she had picked the night before had grown beautiful blossoms of pink and white and she could see, from her window, that the whole tree was covered in blossom, too. Bees flew in and out of the flowers and little birds sang from the topmost boughs.

And Lucy never saw the witch again.

Mouse in the Snow

It was winter and snow covered everything in a thick, white blanket. An owl with huge, outspread wings flew over the white woods, the white fields and over the white roofs of houses. In his claws he held a trembling, small brown mouse.

Mouse, who was feeling very cold as well as very frightened, gave a sudden sneeze. Owl, startled by the noise, dropped Mouse who fell down, down, down until he found himself clinging to a net of bird nuts which hung in a holly tree.

"What a lucky escape," squeaked the surprised mouse, "and what a lot of nuts for one single branch of one tree."

He clung on for all he was worth. "Well, I've never eaten supper up in the air before, but I'll try anything once."

And he nibbled a hole in the net, pulled out a peanut with his front teeth and crunched it.

A sleek, black cat was sitting outside the pointed window of a small house. The window was lit from inside, so only her outline could be seen. When she saw Mouse on the nut bag she gave a yawn of pleasure and flexed her long, sharp claws.

"You will soon get tired of hanging up there," she said. "And when you fall to the ground we will play a little game together."

Her round, yellow eyes shone in the darkness.

Owl, who had flown to a nearby tree, blinked his round, yellow eyes and said nothing.

The small brown mouse had eaten only three nuts when his feet began to get very tired from clinging to the bag. He could not run along the branch because of the prickly holly leaves. Holding his breath, he loosened his hold on the nut bag and fell to the road below. Cat, quick as a flash, leapt towards him, but Mouse darted onto a pile of snow and started burrowing into it.

Cat blinked and hesitated as the flurry of snow settled in cold diamonds on her whiskers. In seconds, Mouse was out of sight and Cat went back to her windowsill making angry, growling noises in her throat.

* * *

In his tunnel under the snow the small mouse felt safe from Cat, and safe from Owl, and very cosy.

"Who would have thought," he squeaked to himself, "that one could be so warm and comfortable inside a heap of snow. I am learning a lot today."

Up above, in the cold night air, Cat was calling to Owl.

"A cat is the cleverest animal in the world," she boasted. "I will soon tempt this silly little mouse from his tunnel. When he climbs out of it I will pounce on him and we will play a little game together. Then, when I get tired of that, I will gobble him up."

Owl in the tree said nothing, but he thought to himself, "Cat thinks she is so clever, but I am a wise old owl. I caught Mouse in the first place. When he climbs out of the snow I will pounce on him before Cat does. I will fly with him to my hole in the oak tree. And then I will gobble him up."

Cat went to the mouth of the tunnel that Mouse had made in the snow and whispered, "Are you there, Mouse? Can you hear me? If you climb out of your tunnel, crawl under the gate and run down the steps you will find yourself in a garden. On the low wall, in the daytime, birds are fed. Grain and nuts are put on the wall, and sometimes cheese. Today the cheese fell into the garden below. There is a big lump of it lying there, half-hidden by the snow. A big lump of rich, Derby cheese, Mouse –

just think of it. But perhaps you are not very hungry?"

Mouse, who had eaten only two berries and three nuts that evening, was feeling so hungry that his tummy rumbled. But he also knew that outside the tunnel was Owl, with his round, yellow eyes and sharp beak, and Cat, with her round, yellow eyes and sharp claws, both waiting to pounce on him and gobble him up.

He thought of the lump of rich, Derby cheese and sighed a little, but said to himself, "Something will turn up. It usually does."

At that moment there was the sound of shouting in the distance. Owl swivelled his head round like a corkscrew. When he saw two boys running up the hill, he gave a loud cry of, "Hoo-hoo! Hoo-hoo!" and flew off into the forest.

The boys stopped by the gate of the house and one picked up a large handful of snow. When Cat saw this she gave an angry miaow and hurried back to her windowsill. The boy made a large snowball and threw it over the wall.

"I can throw further than that," cried the other boy. He, too, picked up a large handful of snow. Inside the snow was Mouse, although the boy did not know it.

Mouse felt the snow being packed all round him until he could hardly breathe. Then he felt himself hurtling through the air at great speed and, with a thud which shook him from tail to whiskers, the snowball landed. The boys went laughing up the hill.

The snowball, which had fallen on the far side of the low garden wall, broke open. Mouse struggled out, feeling rather dazed. He made sure he was the right way up, shook the snow from his whiskers and sniffed the air. And there beside him, half-hidden by snow, was the large lump of Derby cheese.

"Well!" squeaked Mouse to himself. "I have seen the world today and no mistake. I have seen white woods, white fields and the white roofs of houses. I have eaten nuts in the air and made a tunnel under the snow. I have travelled far by Owl and snowball, and soon it will be time to find a hole in the wall and go to sleep. But first I will have a really good supper."

He picked up the large piece of cheese in his front paws, and under the round yellow eye of the *moon* – he gobbled it up!